## DOVER

### CHILDREN'S THRIFT CLASSICS

# Lightfoot the Deer

## THORNTON W. BURGESS

*Illustrations by Harrison Cady*

PUBLISHED IN ASSOCIATION WITH THE
THORNTON W. BURGESS MUSEUM AND THE
GREEN BRIAR NATURE CENTER, SANDWICH, MASSACHUSETTS
BY
DOVER PUBLICATIONS, INC., MINEOLA, NEW YORK

# DOVER CHILDREN'S THRIFT CLASSICS
## EDITOR OF THIS VOLUME: SUSAN L. RATTINER

### Bibliographical Note

This Dover edition, first published in 1998 in association with the Thornton W. Burgess Museum and the Green Briar Nature Center, Sandwich, Massachusetts, who have provided a new introduction, is an unabridged republication of the work first published by Grosset & Dunlap, New York, in 1921. This volume reproduces four original illustrations by Harrison Cady.

### Library of Congress Cataloging-in-Publication Data

Burgess, Thornton W. (Thornton Waldo), 1874–1965.
Lightfoot the deer / Thornton W. Burgess; illustrations by Harrison Cady.
        p.      cm. — (Dover children's thrift classics)
"Published in association with the Thornton W. Burgess Museum and the Green Briar Nature Center, Sandwich, Massachusetts."
Summary: An unabridged republication of the 1921 classic in which Lightfoot encounters animal friends Peter Rabbit, Sammy Jay, Paddy the Beaver and others.
ISBN 0-486-40100-6 (pbk.)
[1. Deer—Fiction. 2. Forest animals—Fiction.] I. Cady, Harrison, 1877– ill. II. Title. III. Series.
PZ7.B917Lg   1998
[Fic]—dc21                                                  97-42201
                                                                CIP
                                                                AC

Manufactured in the United States of America
Dover Publications, Inc., 31 East 2nd Street, Mineola, N.Y. 11501

# Introduction to the Dover Edition

IN THIS TALE, we meet Lightfoot, a graceful and majestic deer who is wandering the Green Forest, proudly displaying his new set of antlers. He leads a happy and peaceful life until the first day of the hunting season. With the help of Paddy Beaver, Sammy Jay, and all his friends who live in the Green Forest, he is able to outwit the hunter who is tracking him. One day Lightfoot hears the sound of hounds coming after him and is forced to leave the security of the Green Forest. After being pursued for many hours, Lightfoot comes to the shore of the Big River where he finds that he is trapped. Tired and exhausted, he summons the last of his energy and swims to the other shore. There, Lightfoot finds a safe haven to wait out the hunting season. On his return to the Green Forest, he finally finds the one thing that makes him happy for the rest of his life.

*Lightfoot the Deer* was originally published in 1921 and is just one of the delightful stories written by children's author Thornton W. Burgess. It was part of the Green Forest Series of four books. These stories first appeared in Burgess's newspaper story column. Mr. Burgess grew up in Sandwich, Massachusetts, on Cape Cod. It is here that he learned a deep appreciation of nature and the outside world. His nature stories have entertained and enlightened children since 1910.

Today, the Thornton W. Burgess Society continues to teach children and adults to appreciate nature through environmental education programming. We encourage you to visit our two facilities, the Thornton W. Burgess Museum and the Green Briar Nature Center in Sandwich. You can also learn more about the Society through our web page at http://www.capecod.net/burgess.

*Wonderfully handsome was Lightfoot the Deer.*

# Illustrations

# Dedication

TO THE MOST BEAUTIFUL OF OUR
FOUR-FOOTED FRIENDS IN THE GREEN FOREST
WITH THE HOPE THAT THIS LITTLE VOLUME
MAY IN SOME DEGREE AID IN THE
PROTECTION OF THE INNOCENT
AND HELPLESS

# Contents

# I

## Peter Rabbit Meets Lightfoot

PETER RABBIT was on his way back from the pond of Paddy the Beaver deep in the Green Forest. He had just seen Mr. and Mrs. Quack start toward the Big River for a brief visit before leaving on their long, difficult journey to the far-away Southland. Farewells are always rather sad, and this particular farewell had left Peter with a lump in his throat—a queer, choky feeling.

"If I were sure that they would return next spring, it wouldn't be so bad," he muttered. "It's those terrible guns. I know what it is to have to watch out for them. Farmer Brown's boy used to hunt me with one of them, but he doesn't any more. But even when he did hunt me it wasn't anything like what the Ducks have to go through. If I kept my eyes and ears open, I could tell when a hunter was coming and could hide in a hole if I wanted to. I never had to worry about my meals. But with the Ducks it is a thousand times worse. They've got to eat while making that long journey, and they can eat only where there is the right kind of food. Hunters with terrible guns know where those places are and hide there until the Ducks come, and the Ducks have no way of knowing whether the hunters are waiting for them or not. That isn't hunting. It's—it's—"

"Well, what is it? What are you talking to yourself about, Peter Rabbit?"

Peter looked up with a start to find the soft, beautiful

eyes of Lightfoot the Deer gazing down at him over the top of a little hemlock tree.

"It's awful," declared Peter. "It's worse than unfair. It doesn't give them any chance at all."

"I suppose it must be so if you say so," replied Lightfoot, "but you might tell me what all this awfulness is about."

Peter grinned. Then he began at the beginning and told Lightfoot all about Mr. and Mrs. Quack and the many dangers they must face on their long journey to the far-away Southland and back again in the spring, all because of the heartless hunters with terrible guns. Lightfoot listened and his great soft eyes were filled with pity for the Quack family.

"I hope they will get through all right," said he, "and I hope they will get back in the spring. It is bad enough to be hunted by men at one time of the year, as no one knows better than I do, but to be hunted in the spring as well as in the fall is more than twice as bad. Men are strange creatures. I do not understand them at all. None of the people of the Green Forest would think of doing such terrible things. I suppose it is quite right to hunt others in order to get enough to eat, though I am thankful to say that I never have had to do that, but to hunt others just for the fun of hunting is something I cannot understand at all. And yet that is what men seem to do it for. I guess the trouble is they never have been hunted themselves and don't know how it feels. Sometimes I think I'll hunt one some day just to teach him a lesson. What are you laughing at, Peter?"

"At the idea of you hunting a man," replied Peter. "Your heart is all right, Lightfoot, but you are too timid and gentle to frighten any one. Big as you are I wouldn't fear you."

With a single swift bound Lightfoot sprang out in

front of Peter. He stamped his sharp hoofs, lowered his handsome head until the sharp points of his antlers, which people call horns, pointed straight at Peter, lifted the hair along the back of his neck, and made a motion as if to plunge at him. His eyes, which Peter had always thought so soft and gentle, seemed to flash fire.

"Oh!" cried Peter in a faint, frightened-sounding voice and leaped to one side before it entered his foolish little head that Lightfoot was just pretending.

Lightfoot chuckled. "Did you say I couldn't frighten any one?" he demanded.

"I—I didn't know you could look so terribly fierce," stammered Peter. "Those antlers look really dangerous when you point them that way. Why—why—what is that hanging to them? It looks like bits of old fur. Have you been tearing somebody's coat, Lightfoot?" Peter's eyes were wide with wonder and suspicion.

## II

## Lightfoot's New Antlers

PETER RABBIT was puzzled. He stared at Lightfoot the Deer a wee bit suspiciously. "Have you been tearing somebody's coat?" he asked again. He didn't like to think it of Lightfoot, whom he always had believed quite as gentle, harmless, and timid as himself. But what else could he think?

Lightfoot slowly shook his head. "No," said he, "I haven't torn anybody's coat."

"Then what are those rags hanging on your antlers?" demanded Peter.

Lightfoot chuckled. "They are what is left of the coverings of my new antlers," he explained.

"What's that? What do you mean by new antlers?" Peter was sitting up very straight, with his eyes fixed on Lightfoot's antlers as though he never had seen them before.

Just what I said," retorted Lightfoot. "What do you think of them? I think they are the finest antlers I've ever had. When I get the rest of those rags off, they will be as handsome a set as ever was grown in the Green Forest."

Lightfoot rubbed his antlers against the trunk of a tree till some of the rags hanging to them dropped off.

Peter blinked very hard. He was trying to understand and he couldn't. Finally he said so.

"What kind of a story are you trying to fill me up with?" he demanded indignantly. "Do you mean to tell me that those are not the antlers that you have had as long as I've known you? How can anything hard like those antlers grow? And if those are new ones, where are the old ones? Show me the old ones, and perhaps I'll believe that these are new ones. The idea of trying to make me believe that antlers grow just like plants! I've seen Bossy the Cow all summer and I know she has got the same horns she had last summer. New antlers indeed!"

"You are quite right, Peter, quite right about Bossy the Cow. She never has new horns, but that isn't any reason why I shouldn't have new antlers, is it?" replied Lightfoot patiently. "Her horns are quite different from my antlers. I have a new pair every year. You haven't seen me all summer, have you, Peter?"

"No, I don't remember that I have," replied Peter, trying very hard to remember when he had last seen Lightfoot.

"I *know* you haven't," retorted Lightfoot. "I know it because I have been hiding in a place you never visit."

"What have you been hiding for?" demanded Peter.

"For my new antlers to grow," replied Lightfoot. "When my new antlers are growing, I want to be away by myself. I don't like to be seen without them or with half-grown ones. Besides, I am very uncomfortable while the new antlers are growing and I want to be alone."

Lightfoot spoke as if he really meant every word he said, but still Peter couldn't, he just *couldn't* believe that those wonderful great antlers had grown out of Lightfoot's head in a single summer. "Where did you leave your old ones and when did they come off?" he asked, and there was doubt in the very tone of his voice.

"They dropped off last spring, but I don't remember

just where," replied Lightfoot. "I was too glad to be rid of them to notice where they dropped. You see they were loose and uncomfortable, and I hadn't any more use for them because I knew that my new ones would be bigger and better. I've got one more point on each than I had last year." Lightfoot began once more to rub his antlers against the tree to get off the queer rags hanging to them and to polish the points. Peter watched in silence for a few minutes. Then, all his suspicions returning, he said:

"But you haven't told me anything about those rags hanging to your antlers."

"And you haven't believed what I have already told you," retorted Lightfoot. "I don't like telling things to people who won't believe me."

## III

# Lightfoot Tells How His Antlers Grew

IT IS HARD to believe what seems impossible. And yet what seems impossible to you may be a very commonplace matter to some one else. So it does not do to say that a thing cannot be possible just because you cannot understand how it can be. Peter Rabbit wanted to believe what Lightfoot the Deer had just told him, but somehow he couldn't. If he had seen those antlers growing, it would have been another matter. But he hadn't seen Lightfoot since the very last of winter, and then Lightfoot had worn just such handsome antlers as he now had. So Peter really couldn't be blamed for not being able to believe that those old ones had been lost and in their place new ones had grown in just the few months of spring and summer.

But Peter didn't blame Lightfoot in the least, because he had told Peter that he didn't like to tell things to people who wouldn't believe what he told them when Peter had asked him about the rags hanging to his antlers. "I'm trying to believe it," he said, quite humbly.

"It's all true," broke in another voice.

Peter jumped and turned to find his big cousin, Jumper the Hare. Unseen and unheard, he had stolen up and had overheard what Peter and Lightfoot had said.

"How do you know it is true?" snapped Peter a little crossly, for Jumper had startled him.

"Because I saw Lightfoot's old antlers after they had

7

fallen off, and I often saw Lightfoot while his new ones were growing," retorted Jumper.

"All right! I'll believe anything that Lightfoot tells me if you say it is true," declared Peter, who greatly admires his cousin, Jumper. "Now tell me about those rags, Lightfoot. Please do."

Lightfoot couldn't resist that "please." "Those rags are what is left of a kind of covering which protected the antlers while they were growing, as I told you before," said he. "Very soon after my old ones dropped off the new ones began to grow. They were not hard, not at all like they are now. They were soft and very tender, and the blood ran through them just as it does through our bodies. They were covered with a sort of skin with hairs on it like thin fur. The ends were not sharply pointed as they now are, but were big and rounded, like knobs. They were not like antlers at all, and they made my head hot and were very uncomfortable. That is why I hid away. They grew very fast, so fast that every day I could see by looking at my reflection in water that they were a little longer. It seemed to me sometimes as if all my strength went into those new antlers. And I had to be very careful not to hit them against anything. In the first place it would have hurt, and in the second place it might have spoiled the shape of them.

"When they had grown to the length you now see, they began to shrink and grow hard. The knobs on the ends shrank until they became pointed. As soon as they stopped growing the blood stopped flowing up in them, and as they became hard they were no longer tender. The skin which had covered them grew dry and split, and I rubbed it off on trees and bushes. The little rags you see are what is left, but I will soon be rid of those. Then I shall be ready to fight if need be and will fear no one save man, and will fear him only when he has a terrible gun with him."

Lightfoot tossed his head proudly and rattled his wonderful antlers against the nearest tree. "Isn't he handsome," whispered Peter to Jumper the Hare; "and did you ever hear of anything so wonderful as the growing of those new antlers in such a short time? It is hard to believe, but I suppose it must be true."

"It is," replied Jumper, "and I tell you, Peter, I would hate to have Lightfoot try those antlers on me, even though I were big as a man. You've always thought of Lightfoot as timid and afraid, but you should see him when he is angry. Few people care to face him then."

# IV

# The Spirit of Fear

When the days grow cold and the nights are clear,
There stalks abroad the spirit of fear.

*Lightfoot the Deer.*

I T IS SAD BUT TRUE. Autumn is often called the sad time of the year, and it *is* the sad time. But it shouldn't be. Old Mother Nature never intended that it should be. She meant it to be the *glad* time. It is the time when all the little people of the Green Forest and the Green Meadows have got over the cares and worries of bringing up families and teaching their children how to look out for themselves. It is the season when food is plentiful, and every one is fat and is, or ought to be, care free. It is the season when Old Mother Nature intended all her little people to be happy, to have nothing to worry them for the little time before the coming of cold weather and the hard times which cold weather always brings.

But instead of this, a grim, dark figure goes stalking over the Green Meadows and through the Green Forest, and it is called the Spirit of Fear. It peers into every hiding-place and wherever it finds one of the little people it sends little cold chills over him, little chills which jolly, round, bright Mr. Sun cannot chase away, though he shine his brightest. All night as well as all day the Spirit of Fear searches out the little people of the Green Meadows and the Green Forest. It will not let them

10

sleep. It will not let them eat in peace. It drives them to seek new hiding-places and then drives them out of those. It keeps them ever ready to fly or run at the slightest sound.

Peter Rabbit was thinking of this as he sat at the edge of the dear Old Briar-patch, looking over to the Green Forest. The Green Forest was no longer just green; it was of many colors, for Old Mother Nature had set Jack Frost to painting the leaves of the maple-trees and the beech-trees, and the birch-trees and the poplar-trees and the chestnut-trees, and he had done his work well. Very, very lovely were the reds and yellows and browns against the dark green of the pines and the spruces and the hemlocks. The Purple Hills were more softly purple than at any other season of the year. It was all very, very beautiful.

But Peter had no thought for the beauty of it all, for the Spirit of Fear had visited even the dear Old Briar-patch, and Peter was afraid. It wasn't fear of Reddy Fox, or Redtail the Hawk, or Hooty the Owl, or Old Man Coyote. They were forever trying to catch him, but they did not strike terror to his heart because he felt quite smart enough to keep out of their clutches. To be sure, they gave him sudden frights sometimes, when they happened to surprise him, but these frights lasted only until he reached the nearest bramble-tangle or hollow log where they could not get at him. But the fear that chilled his heart now never left him even for a moment.

And Peter knew that this same fear was clutching at the hearts of Bob White, hiding in the brown stubble; of Mrs. Grouse, squatting in the thickest bramble-tangle in the Green Forest; of Uncle Billy Possum and Bobby Coon in their hollow trees; of Jerry Muskrat in the Smiling Pool; of Happy Jack Squirrel, hiding in the tree tops; of Lightfoot the Deer, lying in the closest thicket he could find. It was even clutching at the hearts of Granny and Reddy Fox and of great, big Buster Bear. It seemed to Peter that no one was so big or so small that this terrible Spirit of Fear had not searched him out.

Far in the distance sounded a sudden bang. Peter jumped and shivered. He knew that every one else who had heard that bang had jumped and shivered just as he had. It was the season of hunters with terrible guns. It was man who had sent this terrible Spirit of Fear to chill the hearts of the little meadow and forest people at this very time when Old Mother Nature had made all things so beautiful and had intended that they should be happiest and most free from care and worry. It was man who had made the autumn a sad time instead of a glad time, the very saddest time of all the year, when Old Mother Nature had done her best to make it the most beautiful.

"I don't understand these men creatures," said Peter to little Mrs. Peter, as they stared fearfully out from the dear Old Briar-patch. "They seem to find pleasure, actually find pleasure, in trying to kill us. I don't understand them at all. They haven't any hearts. That must be the reason; they haven't any hearts."

*"I don't understand these men creatures,"*
*said Peter to little Mrs. Peter.*

# V

## Sammy Jay Brings Lightfoot Word

SAMMY JAY is one of those who believe in the wisdom of the old saying, "Early to bed and early to rise." Sammy needs no alarm clock to get up early in the morning. He is awake as soon as it is light enough to see and wastes no time wishing he could sleep a little longer. His stomach wouldn't let him if he wanted to. Sammy always wakes up hungry. In this he is no different from all his feathered neighbors.

So the minute Sammy gets his eyes open he makes his toilet, for Sammy is very neat, and starts out to hunt for his breakfast. Long ago Sammy discovered that there is no safer time of day to visit the dooryards of those two-legged creatures called men than very early in the morning. On this particular morning he had planned to fly over to Farmer Brown's dooryard, but at the last minute he changed his mind. Instead, he flew over to the dooryard of another farm. It was so very early in the morning that Sammy didn't expect to find anybody stirring, so you can guess how surprised he was when, just as he came in sight of that dooryard, he saw the door of the house open and a man step out.

Sammy stopped on the top of the nearest tree. "Now what is that man doing up as early as this?" muttered Sammy. Then he caught sight of something under the man's arm. He didn't have to look twice to know what it was. It was a gun! Yes, sir, it was a gun, a terrible gun.

"Ha!" exclaimed Sammy, and quite forgot that his

14

stomach was empty. "Now who can that fellow be after so early in the morning? I wonder if he is going to the dear Old Briar-patch to look for Peter Rabbit, or if he is going to the Old Pasture in search of Reddy Fox, or if it is Mr. and Mrs. Grouse he hopes to kill. I think I'll sit right here and watch."

So Sammy sat in the top of the tree and watched the hunter with the terrible gun. He saw him head straight for the Green Forest. "It's Mr. and Mrs. Grouse after all, I guess," thought Sammy. "If I knew just where they were I'd go over and warn them." But Sammy didn't know just where they were and he knew that it might take him a long time to find them, so he once more began to think of breakfast and then, right then, another thought popped into his head. He thought of Lightfoot the Deer.

Sammy watched the hunter enter the Green Forest, then he silently followed him. From the way the hunter moved, Sammy decided that he wasn't thinking of Mr. and Mrs. Grouse. "It's Lightfoot the Deer, sure as I live," muttered Sammy. "He ought to be warned. He certainly ought to be warned. I know right where he is. I believe I'll warn him myself."

Sammy found Lightfoot right where he had expected to. "He's coming!" cried Sammy. "A hunter with a terrible gun is coming!"

## VI

# A Game of Hide and Seek

THERE WAS a game of hide and seek that Danny Meadow Mouse once played with Buster Bear. It was a very dreadful game for Danny. But hard as it was for Danny, it didn't begin to be as hard as the game Lightfoot the Deer was playing with the hunter in the Green Forest.

In the case of Buster Bear and Danny, the latter had simply to keep out of reach of Buster. As long as Buster didn't get his great paws on Danny, the latter was safe. Then, too, Danny is a very small person. He is so small that he can hide under two or three leaves. Wherever he is, he is pretty sure to find a hiding-place of some sort. His small size gives him advantages in a game of hide and seek. It certainly does. But Lightfoot the Deer is big. He is one of the largest of the people who live in the Green Forest. Being so big, it is not easy to hide.

Moreover, a hunter with a terrible gun does not have to get close in order to kill. Lightfoot knew all this as he waited for the coming of the hunter of whom Sammy Jay had warned him. He had learned many lessons in the hunting season of the year before and he remembered every one of them. He knew that to forget even one of them might cost him his life. So, standing motionless behind a tangle of fallen trees, Lightfoot listened and watched.

Presently over in the distance he heard Sammy Jay screaming, "Thief, thief, thief!" A little sigh of relief escaped Lightfoot. He knew that that screaming of Sammy Jay's was a warning to tell him where the hunter was. Knowing just where the hunter was made it easier for Lightfoot to know what to do.

A Merry Little Breeze came stealing through the Green Forest. It came from behind Lightfoot and danced on towards the hunter with the terrible gun. Instantly Lightfoot began to steal softly away through the Green Forest. He took the greatest care to make no sound. He went in a half-circle, stopping every few steps to listen and test the air with his wonderful nose. Can you guess what Lightfoot was trying to do? He was trying to get behind the hunter so that the Merry Little Breezes would bring to him the dreaded man-scent. So long as Lightfoot could get that scent, he would know where the hunter was, though he could neither see nor hear him. If he had remained where Sammy Jay had found him, the hunter might have come within shooting distance before Lightfoot could have located him.

So the hunter with the terrible gun walked noiselessly through the Green Forest, stepping with the greatest care to avoid snapping a stick underfoot, searching with keen eye every thicket and likely hiding-place for a glimpse of Lightfoot, and studying the ground for traces to show that Lightfoot had been there.

## VII

# The Merry Little Breezes Help Lightfoot

COULD YOU have seen the hunter with the terrible gun and Lightfoot the Deer that morning on which the hunting season opened you might have thought that Lightfoot was hunting the hunter instead of the hunter hunting Lightfoot. You see, Lightfoot was behind the hunter instead of in front of him. He was following the hunter, so as to keep track of him. As long as he knew just where the hunter was, he felt reasonably safe.

The Merry Little Breezes are Lightfoot's best friends. They always bring to him all the different scents they find as they wander through the Green Forest. And Lightfoot's delicate nose is so wonderful that he can take these scents, even though they be very faint, and tell just who or what has made them. So, though he makes the best possible use of his big ears and his beautiful eyes, he trusts more to his nose to warn him of danger. For this reason, during the hunting season when he moves about, he moves in the direction from which the Merry Little Breezes may be blowing. He knows that they will bring to him warning of any danger which may lie in that direction.

Now the hunter with the terrible gun who was looking for Lightfoot knew all this, for he was wise in the ways of Lightfoot and of the other little people of the Green Forest. When he had entered the Green Forest that morning he had first of all made sure of the direction from which the Merry Little Breezes were coming.

Then he had begun to hunt in that direction, knowing that thus his scent would be carried behind him. It is more than likely that he would have reached the hiding-place of Lightfoot the Deer before the latter would have known that he was in the Green Forest, had it not been for Sammy Jay's warning.

When he reached the tangle of fallen trees behind which Lightfoot had been hiding, he worked around it slowly, and with the greatest care, holding his terrible gun ready to use instantly should Lightfoot leap out. Presently he found Lightfoot's footprints in the soft ground and studying them he knew that Lightfoot had known of his coming.

"It was that confounded Jay," muttered the hunter. "Lightfoot heard him and knew what it meant. I know what he has done; he has circled round so as to get behind me and get my scent. It is a clever trick, a very clever trick, but two can play at that game. I'll just try that little trick myself."

So the hunter in his turn made a wide circle back, and presently there was none of the dreaded man-smell among the scents which the Merry Little Breezes brought to Lightfoot. Lightfoot had lost track of the hunter.

## VIII

## Wit Against Wit

IT WAS A dreadful game the hunter with the terrible gun and Lightfoot the Deer were playing in the Green Forest. It was a matching of wit against wit, the hunter seeking to take Lightfoot's life, and Lightfoot seeking to save it. The experience of other years had taught Lightfoot much of the ways of hunters and not one of the things he had learned about them was forgotten. But the hunter in his turn knew much of the ways of Deer. So it was that each was trying his best to out-guess the other.

When the hunter found the hiding-place Lightfoot had left at the warning of Sammy Jay he followed Lightfoot's tracks for a short distance. It was slow work, and only one whose eyes had been trained to notice little things could have done it. You see, there was no snow, and only now and then, when he had stepped on a bit of soft ground, had Lightfoot left a footprint. But there were other signs which the hunter knew how to read,—a freshly upturned leaf here, and here, a bit of moss lightly crushed. These things told the hunter which way Lightfoot had gone.

Slowly, patiently, watchfully, the hunter followed. After a while he stopped with a satisfied grin. "I thought as much," he muttered. "He heard that pesky Jay and circled around so as to get my scent. I'll just cut across to my old trail and unless I am greatly mistaken, I'll find his tracks there."

So, swiftly but silently, the hunter cut across to his old trail, and in a few moments he found just what he expected,—one of Lightfoot's footprints. Once more he grinned.

"Well, old fellow, I've outguessed you this time," said he to himself. "I am behind you and the wind is from you to me, so that you cannot get my scent. I wouldn't be a bit surprised if you're back right where you started from, behind that old windfall." He at once began to move forward silently and cautiously, with eyes and ears alert and his terrible gun ready for instant use.

Now when Lightfoot, following behind the hunter, had lost the scent of the latter, he guessed right away that the latter had found his tracks and had started to follow them. Lightfoot stood still and listened with all his might for some little sound to tell him where the hunter was. But there was no sound and after a little Lightfoot began to move on. He didn't dare remain still, lest the hunter should creep up within shooting distance. There was only one direction in which it was safe for Lightfoot to move, and that was the direction from which the Merry Little Breezes were blowing. So long as they brought him none of the dreaded man-smell, he knew that he was safe. The hunter might be behind him—probably he was—but ahead of him, so long as the Merry Little Breezes were blowing in his face and brought no man-smell, was safety.

## IX

## Lightfoot Becomes Uncertain

LIGHTFOOT THE DEER traveled on through the Green Forest, straight ahead in the direction from which the Merry Little Breezes were blowing. Every few steps he would raise his delicate nose and test all the scents that the Merry Little Breezes were bringing. So long as he kept the Merry Little Breezes blowing in his face, he could be sure whether or not there was danger ahead of him.

Lightfoot uses his nose very much as you and I use our eyes. It tells him the things he wants to know. He knew that Reddy Fox had been along ahead of him, although he didn't get so much as a glimpse of Reddy's red coat. Once he caught just the faintest of scents which caused him to stop abruptly and test the air more carefully than ever. It was the scent of Buster Bear. But it was so very faint that Lightfoot knew Buster was not near, so he went ahead again, but even more carefully than before. After a little he couldn't smell Buster at all, so he knew then that Buster had merely passed that way when he was going to some other part of the Green Forest.

Lightfoot knew that he had nothing to fear in that direction so long as the Merry Little Breezes brought him none of the dreaded man-scent, and he knew that he could trust the Merry Little Breezes to bring him that scent if there should be a man anywhere in front of him. You know the Merry Little Breezes are Lightfoot's

22

best friends. But Lightfoot didn't want to keep going in that direction all day.

It would take him far away from that part of the Green Forest with which he was familiar and which he called home. It might in time take him out of the Green Forest and that wouldn't do at all. So after a while Lightfoot became uncertain. He didn't know just what to do. You see, he couldn't tell whether or not that hunter with the terrible gun was still following him.

Every once in a while he would stop in a thicket of young trees or behind a tangle of fallen trees uprooted by the wind. There he would stand, facing the direction from which he had come, and watch and listen for some sign that the hunter was still following. But after a few minutes of this he would grow uneasy and then bound away in the direction from which the Merry Little Breezes were blowing, so as to be sure of not running into danger.

"If only I could know if that hunter is still following, I would know better what to do," thought Lightfoot. "I've got to find out."

## X

# Lightfoot's Clever Trick

LIGHTFOOT THE DEER is smart. Yes, Sir, Lightfoot the Deer is smart. He has to be, especially in the hunting season, to save his life. If he were not smart he would have been killed long ago. He never makes the foolish mistake of thinking that other people are not smart. He knew that the hunter who had started out to follow him early that morning was not one to be easily discouraged or to be fooled by simple tricks. He had a very great respect for the smartness of that hunter. He knew that he couldn't afford to be careless for one little minute.

The certainty of danger is sometimes easier to bear than the uncertainty of not knowing whether or not there really is any danger. Lightfoot felt that if he could know just where the hunter was, he himself would know better what to do. The hunter might have become discouraged and given up following him. In that case he could rest and stop worrying. It would be better to know that he was being followed than not to know. But how was he to find out? Lightfoot kept turning this over and over in his mind as he traveled through the Green Forest. Then an idea came to him.

"I know what I'll do. I know just what I'll do," said Lightfoot to himself. "I'll find out whether or not that hunter is still following me and I'll get a little rest. Goodness knows, I need a rest."

Lightfoot bounded away swiftly and ran for some distance, then he turned and quickly, but very, very quietly, returned in the direction from which he had just come but a little to one side of his old trail. After a while he saw what he was looking for, a pile of branches which woodchoppers had left when they had trimmed the trees they had cut down. This was near the top of a little hill. Lightfoot went up the hill and stopped behind the pile of brush. For a few moments he stood there perfectly still, looking and listening. Then, with a little sigh of relief, he lay down, where, without being in any danger of being seen himself, he could watch his old trail through the hollow at the bottom of the hill. If the hunter were still following him, he would pass through that hollow in plain sight.

For a long time Lightfoot rested comfortably behind the pile of brush. There was not a suspicious movement or a suspicious sound to show that danger was abroad in the Green Forest. He saw Mr. and Mrs. Grouse fly down across the hollow and disappear among the trees on the other side. He saw Unc' Billy Possum looking over a hollow tree and guessed that Unc' Billy was getting ready to go into winter quarters. He saw Jumper the Hare squat down under a low-hanging branch of a hemlock-tree and prepare to take a nap. He heard Drummer the Woodpecker at work drilling after worms in a tree not far away. Little by little Lightfoot grew easy in his mind. It must be that that hunter had become discouraged and was no longer following him.

# The Hunted Watches the Hunter

Iᴛ ᴡᴀꜱ ꜱᴏ quiet and peaceful and altogether lovely there in the Green Forest, where Lightfoot the Deer lay resting behind a pile of brush near the top of a little hill, that it didn't seem possible such a thing as sudden death could be anywhere near. It didn't seem possible that there could be any need for watchfulness. But Lightfoot long ago had learned that often danger is nearest when it seems least to be expected. So, though he would have liked very much to have taken a nap, Lightfoot was too wise to do anything so foolish. He kept his beautiful, great, soft eyes fixed in the direction from which the hunter with the terrible gun would come if he were still following that trail. He kept his great ears gently moving to catch every little sound.

Lightfoot had about decided that the hunter had given up hunting for that day, but he didn't let this keep him from being any the less watchful. It was better to be overwatchful than the least bit careless. By and by, Lightfoot's keen ears caught the sound of the snapping of a little stick in the distance. It was so faint a sound that you or I would have missed it altogether. But Lightfoot heard it and instantly he was doubly alert, watching in the direction from which that faint sound had come. After what seemed a long, long time he saw something moving, and a moment later a man came into view. It was the hunter and across one arm he carried the terrible gun.

Lightfoot knew now that this hunter had patience and perseverance and had not yet given up hope of getting near enough to shoot Lightfoot. He moved forward slowly, setting each foot down with the greatest care, so as not to snap a stick or rustle the leaves. He was watching sharply ahead, ready to shoot should he catch a glimpse of Lightfoot within range.

Right along through the hollow at the foot of the little hill below Lightfoot the hunter passed. He was no longer studying the ground for Lightfoot's tracks, because the ground was so hard and dry down there that Lightfoot had left no tracks. He was simply hunting in the direction from which the Merry Little Breezes were blowing because he knew that Lightfoot had gone in that direction, and he also knew that if Lightfoot were still ahead of him, his scent could not be carried to Lightfoot. He was doing what is called "hunting up-wind."

Lightfoot kept perfectly still and watched the hunter disappear among the trees. Then he silently got to his feet, shook himself lightly, and noiselessly stole away over the hilltop towards another part of the Green Forest. He felt sure that that hunter would not find him again that day.

## XII

## Lightfoot Visits Paddy the Beaver

DEEP IN THE Green Forest is the pond where lives
Paddy the Beaver. It is Paddy's own pond, for he
made it himself. He made it by building a dam across
the Laughing Brook.

When Lightfoot bounded away through the Green
Forest, after watching the hunter pass through the hollow below him, he remembered Paddy's pond. "That's
where I'll go," thought Lightfoot. "It is such a lonesome
part of the Green Forest that I do not believe that
hunter will come there. I'll just run over and make
Paddy a friendly call."

So Lightfoot bounded along deeper and deeper into
the Green Forest. Presently through the trees he caught
the gleam of water. It was Paddy's pond. Lightfoot
approached it cautiously. He felt sure he was rid of the
hunter who had followed him so far that day, but he
knew that there might be other hunters in the Green
Forest. He knew that he couldn't afford to be careless
for even one little minute. Lightfoot had lived long
enough to know that most of the sad things and dreadful things that happen in the Green Forest and on
the Green Meadows are due to carelessness. No one
who is hunted, be he big or little, can afford ever to be
careless.

Now Lightfoot had known of hunters hiding near
water, hoping to shoot him when he came to drink.
That always seemed to Lightfoot a dreadful thing, an

unfair thing. But hunters had done it before and they might do it again. So Lightfoot was careful to approach Paddy's pond upwind. That is, he approached the side of the pond from which the Merry Little Breezes were blowing toward him, and all the time he kept his nose working. He knew that if any hunters were hidden there, the Merry Little Breezes would bring him their scent and thus warn him.

He had almost reached the edge of Paddy's pond when from the farther shore there came a sudden crash. It startled Lightfoot terribly for just an instant. Then he guessed what it meant. That crash was the falling of a tree. There wasn't enough wind to blow over even the most shaky dead tree. There had been no sound of axes, so he knew it could not have been chopped down by men. It must be that Paddy the Beaver had cut it, and if Paddy had been working in daylight, it was certain that no one had been around that pond for a long time.

So Lightfoot hurried forward eagerly, cautiously. When he reached the bank he looked across towards where the sound of that falling tree had come from; a branch of a tree was moving along in the water and half hidden by it was a brown head. It was Paddy the Beaver taking the branch to his food pile.

## XIII

## Lightfoot and Paddy Become Partners

THE INSTANT Lightfoot saw Paddy the Beaver he knew that for the time being, at least, there was no danger. He knew that Paddy is one of the shyest of all the little people of the Green Forest and that when he is found working in the daytime it means that he has been undisturbed for a long time; otherwise he would work only at night.

Paddy saw Lightfoot almost as soon as he stepped out on the bank. He kept right on swimming with the branch of a poplar-tree until he reached his food pile, which, you know, is in the water. There he forced the branch down until it was held by other branches already sunken in the pond. This done, he swam over to where Lightfoot was watching. "Hello, Lightfoot!" he exclaimed. "You are looking handsomer than ever. How are you feeling these fine autumn days?"

"Anxious," replied Lightfoot. "I am feeling terribly anxious. Do you know what day this is?"

"No," replied Paddy, "I don't know what day it is, and I don't particularly care. It is enough for me that it is one of the finest days we've had for a long time."

"I wish I could feel that way," said Lightfoot wistfully. "I wish I could feel that way, Paddy, but I can't. No, Sir, I can't. You see, this is the first of the most dreadful days in all the year for me. The hunters started looking for me before Mr. Sun was really out of bed. At least one hunter did, and I don't doubt there are others. I fooled

*"My, but that's a beautiful set of antlers you have!"*

that one, but from now to the end of the hunting season there will not be a single moment of daylight when I will feel absolutely safe."

Paddy crept out on the bank and chewed a little twig of poplar thoughtfully. Paddy says he can always think better if he is chewing something. "That's bad news, Lightfoot. I'm sorry to hear it. I certainly am sorry to hear it," said Paddy. "Why anybody wants to hunt such a handsome fellow as you are, I cannot understand. My, but that's a beautiful set of antlers you have!"

"They are the best I've ever had; but do you know, Paddy, I suspect that they may be one of the reasons I am hunted so," replied Lightfoot a little sadly. "Good looks are not always to be desired. Have you seen any hunters around here lately?"

Paddy shook his head. "Not a single hunter," he replied. "I tell you what it is, Lightfoot, let's be partners for a while. You stay right around my pond. If I see or hear or smell anything suspicious, I'll warn you. You do the same for me. Two sets of eyes, ears and noses are better than one. What do you say, Lightfoot?"

"I'll do it," replied Lightfoot.

## XIV

## How Paddy Warned Lightfoot

IT WAS A queer partnership, that partnership between Lightfoot and Paddy, but it was a good partnership. They had been the best of friends for a long time. Paddy had always been glad to have Lightfoot visit his pond. To tell the truth, he was rather fond of handsome Lightfoot. You know Paddy is himself not at all handsome. On land he is a rather clumsy-looking fellow and really homely. So he admired Lightfoot greatly. That is one reason why he proposed that they be partners.

Lightfoot himself thought the idea a splendid one. He spent that night browsing not far from Paddy's pond. With the coming of daylight he lay down in a thicket of young hemlock-trees near the upper end of the pond. It was a quiet, peaceful day. It was so quiet and peaceful and beautiful it was hard to believe that hunters with terrible guns were searching the Green Forest for beautiful Lightfoot. But they were, and Lightfoot knew that sooner or later one of them would be sure to visit Paddy's pond. So, though he rested and took short naps all through that beautiful day, he was anxious. He couldn't help but be.

The next morning found Lightfoot back in the same place. But this morning he took no naps. He rested, but all the time he was watchful and alert. A feeling of uneasiness possessed him. He felt in his bones that danger in the shape of a hunter with a terrible gun was not far distant.

But the hours slipped away, and little by little he grew less uneasy. He began to hope that that day would prove as peaceful as the previous day had been. Then suddenly there was a sharp report from the farther end of Paddy's pond. It was almost like a pistol shot. However, it wasn't a pistol shot. It wasn't a shot at all. It was the slap of Paddy's broad tail on the surface of the water. Instantly Lightfoot was on his feet. He knew just what that meant. He knew that Paddy had seen or heard or smelled a hunter.

It was even so. Paddy had heard a dry stick snap. It was a very tiny snap, but it was enough to warn Paddy. With only his head above water he had watched in the direction from which that sound had come. Presently, stealing quietly along towards the pond, a hunter had come in view. Instantly Paddy had brought his broad tail down on the water with all his force. He knew that Lightfoot would know that that meant danger. Then Paddy had dived, and swimming under water, had sought the safety of his house. He had done his part, and there was nothing more he could do.

# The Three Watchers

WHEN PADDY the Beaver slapped the water with his broad tail, making a noise like a pistol shot, Lightfoot understood that this was meant as a warning of danger. He was on his feet instantly, with eyes, ears and nose seeking the cause of Paddy's warning. After a moment or two he stole softly up to the top of a little ridge some distance back from Paddy's pond, but from the top of which he could see the whole of the pond. There he hid among some close-growing young hemlock-trees. It wasn't long before he saw a hunter with a terrible gun come down to the shore of the pond.

Now the hunter had heard Paddy slap the water with his broad tail. Of course. There would have been something very wrong with his ears had he failed to hear it.

"Confound that Beaver!" muttered the hunter crossly. "If there was a Deer anywhere around this pond, he probably is on his way now. I'll have a look around and see if there are any signs."

So the hunter went on to the edge of Paddy's pond and then began to walk around it, studying the ground as he walked. Presently he found the footprints of Lightfoot in the mud where Lightfoot had gone down to the pond to drink.

"I thought as much," muttered the hunter. "Those tracks were made last night. That Deer probably was lying down somewhere near here, and I might have had a shot but for that pesky Beaver. I'll just look the land over, and then I think I'll wait here awhile. If that Deer isn't too badly scared, he may come back."

So the hunter went quite around the pond, looking into all likely hiding-places. He found where Lightfoot had been lying, and he knew that in all probability Lightfoot had been there when Paddy gave the danger signal.

"It's of no use for me to try to follow him," thought the hunter. "It is too dry for me to track him. He may not be so badly scared, after all. I'll just find a good place and wait."

So the hunter found an old log behind some small trees and there sat down. He could see all around Paddy's pond. He sat perfectly still. He was a clever hunter and he knew that so long as he did not move he was not likely to be noticed by any sharp eyes that might come that way. What he didn't know was that Lightfoot had been watching him all the time and was even then standing where he could see him. And another thing he didn't know was that Paddy the Beaver had come out of his house and, swimming under water, had reached a hiding-place on the opposite shore from which he too had seen the hunter sit down on the log.

So the hunter watched for Lightfoot, and Lightfoot and Paddy watched the hunter.

# Visitors to Paddy's Pond

THAT HUNTER was a man of patience. Also he was a man who understood the little people of the Green Forest and the Green Meadows. He knew that if he would not be seen he must not move. So he didn't move. He kept as motionless as if he were a part of the very log on which he was sitting.

For some time there was no sign of any living thing. Then, from over the tree tops in the direction of the Big River, came the whistle of swift wings, and Mr. and Mrs. Quack alighted with a splash in the pond. For a few moments they sat on the water, a picture of watchful suspicion. They were looking and listening to make sure that no danger was near. Satisfied at last, they began to clean their feathers. It was plain that they felt safe. Paddy the Beaver was tempted to warn them that they were not as safe as they thought, but as long as the hunter did not move Paddy decided to wait.

Now the hunter was sorely tempted to shoot these Ducks, but he knew that if he did he would have no chance that day to get Lightfoot the Deer, and it was Lightfoot he wanted. So Mr. and Mrs. Quack swam about within easy range of that terrible gun without once suspecting that danger was anywhere near.

By and by the hunter's keen eyes caught a movement at one end of Paddy's dam. An instant later Bobby Coon appeared. It was clear that Bobby was quite unsuspicious. He carried something, but just what the hunter

could not make out. He took it down to the edge of the
water and there carefully washed it. Then he climbed
up on Paddy's dam and began to eat. You know Bobby
Coon is very particular about his food. Whenever there
is water near, Bobby washes his food before eating.
Once more the hunter was tempted, but did not yield to
the temptation, which was a very good thing for Bobby
Coon.

All this Lightfoot saw as he stood among the little
hemlock-trees at the top of the ridge behind the hunter.
He saw and he understood. "It is because he wants to
kill me that he doesn't shoot at Mr. and Mrs. Quack or
Bobby Coon," thought Lightfoot a little bitterly. "What
have I ever done that he should be so anxious to kill
me?"

Still the hunter sat without moving. Mr. and Mrs.
Quack contentedly hunted for food in the mud at the
bottom of Paddy's pond. Bobby Coon finished his meal,
crossed the dam and disappeared in the Green Forest.
He had gone off to take a nap somewhere. Time slipped
away. The hunter continued to watch patiently for
Lightfoot, and Lightfoot and Paddy the Beaver watched
the hunter. Finally, another visitor appeared at the
upper end of the pond—a visitor in a wonderful coat of
red. It was Reddy Fox.

## XVII

# Sammy Jay Arrives

WHEN REDDY FOX arrived at the pond of Paddy the Beaver, the hunter who was hiding there saw him instantly. So did Lightfoot. But no one else did. He approached in that cautious, careful way that he always uses when he is hunting. The instant he reached a place where he could see all over Paddy's pond, he stopped as suddenly as if he had been turned to stone. He stopped with one foot lifted in the act of taking a step. He had seen Mr. and Mrs. Quack.

Now you know there is nothing Reddy Fox likes better for a dinner than a Duck. The instant he saw Mr. and Mrs. Quack, a gleam of longing crept into his eyes and his mouth began to water. He stood motionless until both Mr. and Mrs. Quack had their heads under water as they searched for food in the mud in the bottom of the pond. Then like a red flash he bounded out of sight behind the dam of Paddy the Beaver.

Presently the hunter saw Reddy's black nose at the end of the dam as Reddy peeped around it to watch Mr. and Mrs. Quack. The latter were slowly moving along in that direction as they fed. Reddy was quick to see this. If he remained right where he was, and Mr. and Mrs. Quack kept on feeding in that direction, the chances were that he would have a dinner of fat Duck. All he need do was to be patient and wait. So, with his eyes fixed fast on Mr. and Mrs. Quack, Reddy Fox crouched behind Paddy's dam and waited.

Watching Reddy and the Ducks, the hunter almost forgot Lightfoot the Deer. Mr. and Mrs. Quack were getting very near to where Reddy was waiting for them. The hunter was tempted to get up and frighten those Ducks. He didn't want Reddy Fox to have them, because he hoped some day to get them himself.

"I suppose," thought he, "I was foolish not to shoot them when I had the chance. They are too far away now, and it looks very much as if that red rascal will get one of them. I believe I'll spoil that red scamp's plans by frightening them away. I don't believe that Deer will be back here to-day anyway, so I may as well save those Ducks."

But the hunter did nothing of the kind. You see, just as he was getting ready to step out from his hiding-place, Sammy Jay arrived. He perched in a tree close to the end of Paddy's dam and at once he spied Reddy Fox. It didn't take him a second to discover what Reddy was hiding there for. "Thief, thief, thief!" screamed Sammy, and then looked down at Reddy with a mischievous look in his sharp eyes. There is nothing Sammy Jay delights in more than in upsetting the plans of Reddy Fox. At the sound of Sammy's voice, Mr. and Mrs. Quack swam hurriedly towards the middle of the pond. They knew exactly what that warning meant. Reddy Fox looked up at Sammy Jay and snarled angrily. Then, knowing it was useless to hide longer, he bounded away through the Green Forest to hunt elsewhere.

# XVIII

# The Hunter Loses His Temper

THE HUNTER, hidden near the pond of Paddy the Beaver, chuckled silently. That is to say, he laughed without making any sound. The hunter thought the warning of Mr. and Mrs. Quack by Sammy Jay was a great joke on Reddy. To tell the truth, he was very much pleased. As you know, he wanted those Ducks himself. He suspected that they would stay in that little pond for some days, and he planned to return there and shoot them after he had got Lightfoot the Deer. He wanted to get Lightfoot first, and he knew that to shoot at anything else might spoil his chance of getting a shot at Lightfoot.

"Sammy Jay did me a good turn," thought the hunter, "although he doesn't know it. Reddy Fox certainly would have caught one of those Ducks had Sammy not come along just when he did. It would have been a shame to have had one of them caught by that Fox. I mean to get one, and I hope both of them, myself."

Now when you come to think of it, it would have been a far greater shame for the hunter to have killed Mr. and Mrs. Quack than for Reddy Fox to have done so. Reddy was hunting them because he was hungry. The hunter would have shot them for sport. He didn't need them. He had plenty of other food. Reddy Fox doesn't kill just for the pleasure of killing.

So the hunter continued to sit in his hiding-place with very friendly feelings for Sammy Jay. Sammy watched Reddy Fox disappear and then flew over to that side of the pond where the hunter was. Mr. and Mrs. Quack called their thanks to Sammy, to which he replied, that he had done no more for them than he would do for anybody, or than they would have done for him.

For some time Sammy sat quietly in the top of the tree, but all the time his sharp eyes were very busy. By and by he spied the hunter sitting on the log. At first he couldn't make out just what it was he was looking at. It didn't move, but nevertheless Sammy was suspicious. Presently he flew over to a tree where he could see better. Right away he spied the terrible gun, and he knew just what that was. Once more he began to yell, "Thief! thief! thief!" at the top of his lungs. It was then that the hunter lost his temper. He knew that now he had been discovered by Sammy Jay, and it was useless to remain there longer. He was angry clear through.

# XIX

## Sammy Jay Is Modest

A s soon as the angry hunter with the terrible gun had disappeared among the trees of the Green Forest, and Lightfoot was sure that he had gone for good, Lightfoot came out from his hiding-place on top of the ridge and walked down to the pond of Paddy the Beaver for a drink. He knew that it was quite safe to do so, for Sammy Jay had followed the hunter, all the time screaming, "Thief! thief! thief!" Every one within hearing could tell just where that hunter was by Sammy's voice. It kept growing fainter and fainter, and by that Lightfoot knew that the hunter was getting farther and farther away.

Paddy the Beaver swam out from his hiding-place and climbed out on the bank near Lightfoot. There was a twinkle in his eyes. "That blue-coated mischief-maker isn't such a bad fellow at heart, after all, is he?" said he.

Lightfoot lifted his beautiful head and set his ears forward to catch the sound of Sammy's voice in the distance.

"Sammy Jay may be a mischief-maker, as some people say," said he, "but you can always count on him to prove a true friend in time of danger. He brought me warning of the coming of the hunter the other morning. You saw him save Mr. and Mrs. Quack a little while ago, and then he actually drove that hunter away. I suppose Sammy Jay has saved more lives than any one I know of. I wish he would come back here and let me thank him."

43

Some time later Sammy Jay did come back. "Well," said he, as he smoothed his feathers, "I chased that fellow clear to the edge of the Green Forest, so I guess there will be nothing more to fear from him to-day. I'm glad to see he hasn't got you yet, Lightfoot. I've been a bit worried about you."

"Sammy," said Lightfoot, "you are one of the best friends I have. I don't know how I can ever thank you for what you have done for me."

"Don't try," replied Sammy shortly. "I haven't done anything but what anybody else would have done. Old Mother Nature gave me a pair of good eyes and a strong voice. I simply make the best use of them I can. Just to see a hunter with a terrible gun makes me angry clear through. I'd rather spoil his hunting than eat."

"You want to watch out, Sammy. One of these days a hunter will lose his temper and shoot you, just to get even with you," warned Paddy the Beaver.

"Don't worry about me," replied Sammy. "I know just how far those terrible guns can shoot, and I don't take any chances. By the way, Lightfoot, the Green Forest is full of hunters looking for you. I've seen a lot of them, and I know they are looking for you because they do not shoot at anybody else even when they have a chance."

## XX

# Lightfoot Hears a Dreadful Sound

D<small>AY AFTER DAY</small>, Lightfoot the Deer played hide and seek for his life with the hunters who were seeking to kill him. He saw them many times, though not one of them saw him. More than once a hunter passed close to Lightfoot's hiding-place without once suspecting it.

But poor Lightfoot was feeling the strain. He was growing thin, and he was so nervous that the falling of a dead leaf from a tree would startle him. There is nothing quite so terrible as being continually hunted. It was getting so that Lightfoot half expected a hunter to step out from behind every tree. Only when the Black Shadows wrapped the Green Forest in Darkness did he know a moment of peace. And those hours of safety were filled with dread of what the next day might bring.

Early one morning a terrible sound rang through the Green Forest and brought Lightfoot to his feet with a startled jump. It was the baying of hounds following a trail. At first it did not sound so terrible. Lightfoot had often heard it before. Many times he had listened to the baying of Bowser the Hound, as he followed Reddy Fox. It had not sounded so terrible then because it meant no danger to Lightfoot.

At first, as he listened early that morning, he took it for granted that those hounds were after Reddy, and so, though startled, he was not worried. But suddenly a dreadful suspicion came to him and he grew more and more anxious as he listened. In a few minutes there was

45

no longer any doubt in his mind. Those hounds were following his trail. It was then that the sound of that baying became terrible. He must run for his life! Those hounds would give him no rest. And he knew that in running from them, he would no longer be able to watch so closely for the hunters with terrible guns. He would no longer be able to hide in thickets. At any time he might be driven right past one of those hunters.

Lightfoot bounded away with such leaps as only Lightfoot can make. In a little while the voices of the hounds grew fainter. Lightfoot stopped to get his breath and stood trembling as he listened. The baying of the hounds again grew louder and louder. Those wonderful noses of theirs were following his trail without the least difficulty. In a panic of fear, Lightfoot bounded away again. As he crossed an old road, the Green Forest rang with the roar of a terrible gun. Something tore a strip of bark from the trunk of a tree just above Lightfoot's back. It was a bullet and it had just missed Lightfoot. It added to his terror and this in turn added to his speed.

So Lightfoot ran and ran, and behind him the voices of the hounds continued to ring through the Green Forest.

# XXI

# How Lightfoot Got Rid of the Hounds

P OOR LIGHTFOOT! It seemed to him that there were no such things as justice and fair play. Had it been just one hunter at a time against whom he had to match his wits it would not have been so bad. But there were many hunters with terrible guns looking for him, and in dodging one he was likely at any time to meet another. This in itself seemed terribly unfair and unjust. But now, added to this was the greater unfairness of being trailed by hounds.

Do you wonder that Lightfoot thought of men as utterly heartless? You see, he could not know that those hounds had not been put on his trail, but had left home to hunt for their own pleasure. He could not know that it was against the law to hunt him with dogs. But though none of those hunters looking for him were guilty of having put the hounds on his trail, each one of them was willing and eager to take advantage of the fact that the hounds were on his trail. Already he had been shot at once and he knew that he would be shot at again if he should be driven where a hunter was hidden.

The ground was damp and scent always lies best on damp ground. This made it easy for the hounds to follow him with their wonderful noses. Lightfoot tried every trick he could think of to make those hounds lose the scent.

"If only I could make them lose it long enough for me

47

to get a little rest, it would help," panted Lightfoot, as he paused for just an instant to listen to the baying of the hounds.

But he couldn't. They allowed him no rest. He was becoming very, very tired. He could no longer bound lightly over fallen logs or brush, as he had done at first. His lungs ached as he panted for breath. He realized that even though he should escape the hunters he would meet an even more terrible death unless he could get rid of those hounds. There would come a time when he would have to stop. Then those hounds would catch up with him and tear him to pieces.

It was then that he remembered the Big River. He turned towards it. It was his only chance and he knew it. Straight through the Green Forest, out across the Green Meadows to the bank of the Big River, Lightfoot ran. For just a second he paused to look behind. The hounds were almost at his heels. Lightfoot hesitated no longer but plunged into the Big River and began to swim. On the banks the hounds stopped and bayed their disappointment, for they did not dare follow Lightfoot out into the Big River.

## XXII

# Lightfoot's Long Swim

THE BIG RIVER was very wide. It would have been a long swim for Lightfoot had he been fresh and at his best. Strange as it may seem, Lightfoot is a splendid swimmer, despite his small, delicate feet. He enjoys swimming.

But now Lightfoot was terribly tired from his long run ahead of the hounds. For a time he swam rapidly, but those weary muscles grew still more weary, and by the time he reached the middle of the Big River it seemed to him that he was not getting ahead at all. At first he had tried to swim towards a clump of trees he could see on the opposite bank above the point where he had entered the water, but to do this he had to swim against the current and he soon found that he hadn't the strength to do this. Then he turned and headed for a point down the Big River. This made the swimming easier, for the current helped him instead of hindering him.

Even then he could feel his strength leaving him. Had he escaped those hounds and the terrible hunters only to be drowned in the Big River? This new fear gave him more strength for a little while. But it did not last long. He was three fourths of the way across the Big River but still that other shore seemed a long distance away. Little by little hope died in the heart of Lightfoot the Deer. He would keep on just as long as he could and then,—well, it was better to drown than to be torn to pieces by dogs.

Just as Lightfoot felt that he could not take another stroke and that the end was at hand, one foot touched something. Then, all four feet touched. A second later he had found solid footing and was standing with the water only up to his knees. He had found a little sand bar out in the Big River. With a little gasp of returning hope, Lightfoot waded along until the water began to grow deeper again. He had hoped that he would be able to wade ashore, but he saw now that he would have to swim again.

So for a long time he remained right where he was. He was so tired that he trembled all over, and he was as frightened as he was tired. He knew that standing out there in the water he could be seen for a long distance, and that made him nervous and fearful. Supposing a hunter on the shore he was trying to reach should see him. Then he would have no chance at all, for the hunter would simply wait for him and shoot him as he came out of the water.

But rest he must, and so he stood for a long time on the little sand bar in the Big River. And little by little he felt his strength returning.

## XXIII

# Lightfoot Finds a Friend

As Lightfoot rested, trying to recover his breath, out there on the little sand bar in the Big River, his great, soft, beautiful eyes watched first one bank and then the other. On the bank he had left, he could see two black-and-white specks moving about, and across the water came the barking of dogs. Those two specks were the hounds who had driven him into the Big River. They were barking now, instead of baying. Presently a brown form joined the black-and-white specks. It was a hunter drawn there by the barking of the dogs. He was too far away to be dangerous, but the mere sight of him filled Lightfoot with terror again. He watched the hunter walk along the bank and disappear in the bushes.

Presently out of the bushes came a boat, and in it was the hunter. He headed straight towards Lightfoot, and then Lightfoot knew that his brief rest was at an end. He must once more swim or be shot by the hunter in the boat. So Lightfoot again struck out for the shore. His rest had given him new strength, but still he was very, very tired and swimming was hard work.

Slowly, oh so slowly, he drew nearer to the bank. What new dangers might be waiting there, he did not know. He had never been on that side of the Big River. He knew nothing of the country on that side. But the uncertainty was better than the certainty behind him. He could hear the sound of the oars as the hunter in the

51

boat did his best to get to him before he should reach the shore.

On Lightfoot struggled. At last he felt bottom beneath his feet. He staggered up through some bushes along the bank and then for an instant it seemed to him his heart stopped beating. Right in front of him stood a man. He had come out into the back yard of the home of that man. It is doubtful which was the more surprised, Lightfoot or the man. Right then and there Lightfoot gave up in despair. He couldn't run. It was all he could do to walk. The long chase by the hounds on the other side of the Big River and the long swim across the Big River had taken all his strength.

Not a spark of hope remained to Lightfoot. He simply stood still and trembled, partly with fear and partly with weariness. Then a surprising thing happened. The man spoke softly. He advanced, not threateningly but slowly, and in a friendly way. He walked around back of Lightfoot and then straight towards him. Lightfoot walked on a few steps, and the man followed, still talking softly. Little by little he urged Lightfoot on, driving him towards an open shed in which was a pile of hay. Without understanding just how, Lightfoot knew that he had found a friend. So he entered the open shed and with a long sigh lay down in the soft hay.

## XXIV

# The Hunter Is Disappointed

HOW HE KNEW he was safe, Lightfoot the Deer couldn't have told you. He just knew it, that was all. He couldn't understand a word said by the man in whose yard he found himself when he climbed the bank after his long swim across the Big River. But he didn't have to understand words to know that he had found a friend. So he allowed the man to drive him gently over to an open shed where there was a pile of soft hay and there he lay down, so tired that it seemed to him he couldn't move another step.

It was only a few minutes later that the hunter who had followed Lightfoot across the River reached the bank and scrambled out of his boat. Lightfoot's friend was waiting just at the top of the bank. Of course the hunter saw him at once.

"Hello, Friend!" cried the hunter. "Did you see a Deer pass this way a few minutes ago? He swam across the river, and if I know anything about it he's too tired to travel far now. I've been hunting that fellow for several days, and if I have any luck at all I ought to get him this time."

"I'm afraid you won't have any luck at all," said Lightfoot's friend. "You see, I don't allow any hunting on my land."

The hunter looked surprised, and then his surprise gave way to anger. "You mean," said he, "that you intend to get that Deer yourself."

Lightfoot's friend shook his head. "No," said he, "I don't mean anything of the kind. I mean that that Deer is not to be killed if I can prevent it, and while it is on my land, I think I can. The best thing for you to do, my friend, is to get into your boat and row back where you came from. Are those your hounds barking over there?"

"No," replied the hunter promptly. "I know the law just as well as you do, and it is against the law to hunt Deer with dogs. I don't even know who owns those two hounds over there."

"That may be true," replied Lightfoot's friend. "I don't doubt it is true. But you are willing to take advantage of the fact that the dogs of some one else have broken the law. You knew that those dogs had driven that Deer into the Big River and you promptly took advantage of the fact to try to reach that Deer before he could get across. You are not hunting for the pleasure of hunting but just to kill. You don't know the meaning of justice or fairness. Now get off my land. Get back into your boat and off my land as quick as you can. That Deer is not very far from here and so tired that he cannot move. Just as long as he will stay here, he will be safe, and I hope he will stay until this miserable hunting season is ended. Now go."

Muttering angrily, the hunter got back into his boat and pushed off, but he didn't row back across the river.

## XXV

# The Hunter Lies in Wait

IF EVER THERE was an angry hunter, it was the one who had followed Lightfoot the Deer across the Big River. When he was ordered to get off the land where Lightfoot had climbed out, he got back into his boat, but he didn't row back to the other side. Instead, he rowed down the river, finally landing on the same side but on land which Lightfoot's friend did not own.

"When that Deer has become rested he'll become uneasy," thought the hunter. "He won't stay on that man's land. He'll start for the nearest woods. I'll go up there and wait for him. I'll get that Deer if only to spite that fellow back there who drove me off. Had it not been for him, I'd have that Deer right now. He was too tired to have gone far. He's got the handsomest pair of antlers I've seen for years. I can sell that head of his for a good price."

So the hunter tied his boat to a tree and once more climbed out. He climbed up the bank and studied the land. Across a wide meadow he could see a brushy old pasture and back of that some thick woods. He grinned.

"That's where that Deer will head for," he decided. "There isn't any other place for him to go. All I've got to do is be patient and wait."

So the hunter took his terrible gun and tramped across the meadow to the brush-grown pasture. There he hid among the bushes where he could peep out and watch the land of Lightfoot's friend. He was still angry because he had been prevented from shooting Lightfoot. At the same time he chuckled, because he thought himself very smart. Lightfoot couldn't possibly reach the shelter of the woods without giving him a shot, and he hadn't the least doubt that Lightfoot would start for the woods just as soon as he felt able to travel. So he made himself comfortable and prepared to wait the rest of the day, if necessary.

Now Lightfoot's friend who had driven the hunter off had seen him row down the river and he had guessed just what was in that hunter's mind. "We'll fool him," said he, chuckling to himself, as he walked back towards the shed where poor Lightfoot was resting.

He did not go too near Lightfoot, for he did not want to alarm him. He just kept within sight of Lightfoot, paying no attention to him but going about his work. You see, this man loved and understood the little people of the Green Forest and the Green Meadows, and he knew that there was no surer way of winning Lightfoot's confidence and trust than by appearing to take no notice of him. Lightfoot, watching him, understood. He knew that this man was a friend and would do him no harm. Little by little, the wonderful, blessed feeling of safety crept over Lightfoot. No hunter could harm him here.

## XXVI

# Lightfoot Does the Wise Thing

ALL THE REST of that day the hunter with the terrible gun lay hidden in the bushes of the pasture where he could watch for Lightfoot the Deer to leave the place of safety he had found. It required a lot of patience on the part of the hunter, but the hunter had plenty of patience. It sometimes seems as if hunters have more patience than any other people.

But this hunter waited in vain. Jolly, round, red Mr. Sun sank down in the west to his bed behind the Purple Hills. The Black Shadows crept out and grew blacker. One by one the stars began to twinkle. Still the hunter waited, and still there was no sign of Lightfoot. At last it became so dark that it was useless for the hunter to remain longer. Disappointed and once more becoming angry, he tramped back to the Big River, climbed into his boat and rowed across to the other side. Then he tramped home and his thoughts were very bitter. He knew that he could have shot Lightfoot had it not been for the man who had protected the Deer. He even began to suspect that this man had himself killed Lightfoot, for he had been sure that as soon as he had become rested Lightfoot would start for the woods, and Lightfoot had done nothing of the kind. In fact, the hunter had not had so much as another glimpse of Lightfoot.

The reason that the hunter had been so disappointed was that Lightfoot was smart. He was smart enough to understand that the man who was saving him from the hunter had done it because he was a true friend. All the afternoon Lightfoot had rested on a bed of soft hay in an open shed and had watched this man going about his work and taking the utmost care to do nothing to frighten Lightfoot.

"He not only will let no one else harm me, but he himself will not harm me," thought Lightfoot. "As long as he is near, I am safe. I'll stay right around here until the hunting season is over, then I'll swim back across the Big River to my home in the dear Green Forest."

So all afternoon Lightfoot rested and did not so much as put his nose outside that open shed. That is why the hunter got no glimpse of him. When it became dark, so dark that he knew there was no longer danger, Lightfoot got up and stepped out under the stars. He was feeling quite himself again. His splendid strength had returned. He bounded lightly across the meadow and up into the brushy pasture where the hunter had been hidden. There and in the woods back of the pasture he browsed, but at the first hint of the coming of another day, Lightfoot turned back, and when his friend, the farmer, came out early in the morning to milk the cows, there was Lightfoot back in the open shed. The farmer smiled. "You are as wise as you are handsome, old fellow," said he.

# XXVII

# Sammy Jay Worries

IT ISN'T often Sammy Jay worries about anybody but himself. Truth to tell, he doesn't worry about himself very often. You see, Sammy is smart, and he knows he is smart. Under that pointed cap of his are some of the cleverest wits in all the Green Forest. Sammy seldom worries about himself because he feels quite able to take care of himself.

But Sammy Jay was worrying now. He was worrying about Lightfoot the Deer. Yes, Sir, Sammy Jay was worrying about Lightfoot the Deer. For two days he had been unable to find Lightfoot or any trace of Lightfoot. But he did find plenty of hunters with terrible guns. It seemed to him that they were everywhere in the Green Forest. Sammy began to suspect that one of them must have succeeded in killing Lightfoot the Deer.

Sammy knew all of Lightfoot's hiding-places. He visited every one of them. Lightfoot wasn't to be found, and no one whom Sammy met had seen Lightfoot for two days.

Sammy felt badly. You see, he was very fond of Lightfoot. You remember it was Sammy who warned Lightfoot of the coming of the hunter on the morning when the dreadful hunting season began. Ever since the hunting season had opened, Sammy had done his best to make trouble for the hunters. Whenever he had found one of them he had screamed at the top of his voice to warn every one within hearing just where that hunter was. Once a hunter had lost his temper and shot at Sammy, but Sammy had suspected that something of the kind might happen, and he had taken care to keep just out of reach.

Sammy had known all about the chasing of Lightfoot by the hounds. Everybody in the Green Forest had known about it. You see, everybody had heard the voices of those hounds. Once, Lightfoot had passed right under the tree in which Sammy was sitting, and a few moments later the two hounds had passed with their noses to the ground as they followed Lightfoot's trail. That was the last Sammy had seen of Lightfoot. He had been able to save Lightfoot from the hunters, but he couldn't save him from the hounds.

The more Sammy thought things over, the more he worried. "I am afraid those hounds drove him out where a hunter could get a shot and kill him, or else that they tired him out and killed him themselves," thought Sammy. "If he were alive, somebody certainly would have seen him and nobody has, since the day those hounds chased him. I declare, I have quite lost my appetite worrying about him. If Lightfoot is dead, and I am almost sure he is, the Green Forest will never seem the same."

## XXVIII

# The Hunting Season Ends

THE VERY worst things come to an end at last. No matter how bad a thing is, it cannot last forever. So it was with the hunting season for Lightfoot the Deer. There came a day when the law protected all Deer,—a day when the hunters could no longer go searching for Lightfoot.

Usually there was great rejoicing among the little people of the Green Forest and the Green Meadows when the hunting season ended and they knew that Lightfoot would be in no more danger until the next hunting season. But this year there was no rejoicing. You see, no one could find Lightfoot. The last seen of him was when he was running for his life with two hounds baying on his trail and the Green Forest filled with hunters watching for a chance to shoot him.

Sammy Jay had hunted everywhere through the Green Forest. Blacky the Crow, whose eyes are quite as sharp as those of Sammy Jay, had joined in the search. They had found no trace of Lightfoot. Paddy the Beaver said that for three days Lightfoot had not visited his pond for a drink. Billy Mink, who travels up and down the Laughing Brook, had looked for Lightfoot's footprints in the soft earth along the banks and had found only old ones. Jumper the Hare had visited Lightfoot's favorite eating places at night, but Lightfoot had not been in any of them.

"I tell you what it is," said Sammy Jay to Bobby Coon,

"something has happened to Lightfoot. Either those hounds caught him and killed him, or he was shot by one of those hunters. The Green Forest will never be the same without him. I don't think I shall want to come over here very much. There isn't one of all the other people who live in the Green Forest who would be missed as Lightfoot will be."

Bobby Coon nodded. "That's true, Sammy," said he. "Without Lightfoot, the Green Forest will never be the same. He never harmed anybody. Why those hunters should have been so anxious to kill one so beautiful is something I can't understand. For that matter, I don't understand why they want to kill any of us. If they really needed us for food, it would be a different matter, but they don't. Have you been up in the Old Pasture and asked Old Man Coyote if he has seen anything of Lightfoot?"

Sammy nodded. "I've been up there twice," said he. "Old Man Coyote has been lying very low during the days, but nights he has done a lot of traveling. You know Old Man Coyote has a mighty good nose, but not once since the day those hounds chased Lightfoot has he found so much as a tiny whiff of Lightfoot's scent. I thought he might have found the place where Lightfoot was killed, but he hasn't, although he has looked for it. Well, the hunting season for Lightfoot is over, but I am afraid it has ended too late."

*"I tell you what it is,"* said Sammy Jay to Bobby Coon,
*"something has happened to Lightfoot."*

XXIX

# Mr. and Mrs. Quack Are Startled

IT WAS THE evening of the day after the closing of the hunting season for Lightfoot the Deer. Jolly, round, red Mr. Sun had gone to bed behind the Purple Hills, and the Black Shadows had crept out across the Big River. Mr. and Mrs. Quack were getting their evening meal among the brown stalks of the wild rice along the edge of the Big River. They took turns in searching for the rice grains in the mud. While Mrs. Quack tipped up and seemed to stand on her head as she searched in the mud for rice, Mr. Quack kept watch for possible danger. Then Mrs. Quack took her turn at keeping watch, while Mr. Quack stood on his head and hunted for rice.

It was wonderfully quiet and peaceful. There was not even a ripple on the Big River. It was so quiet that they could hear the barking of a dog at a farmhouse a mile away. They were far enough out from the bank to have nothing to fear from Reddy Fox or Old Man Coyote. So they had nothing to fear from any one save Hooty the Owl. It was for Hooty that they took turns in watching. It was just the hour when Hooty likes best to hunt.

By and by they heard Hooty's hunting call. It was far away in the Green Forest. Then Mr. and Mrs. Quack felt easier, and they talked in low, contented voices. They felt that for a while at least there was nothing to fear.

Suddenly a little splash out in the Big River caught Mr. Quack's quick ear. As Mrs. Quack brought her head up out of the water, Mr. Quack warned her to keep quiet. Noiselessly they swam among the brown stalks until they could see out across the Big River. There was another little splash out there in the middle. It wasn't the splash made by a fish; it was a splash made by something much bigger than any fish. Presently they made out a silver line moving towards them from the Black Shadows. They knew exactly what it meant. It meant that some one was out there in the Big River moving towards them. Could it be a boat containing a hunter?

With their necks stretched high, Mr. and Mrs. Quack watched. They were ready to take to their strong wings the instant they discovered danger. But they did not want to fly until they were sure that it *was* danger approaching. They were startled, very much startled.

Presently they made out what looked like the branch of a tree moving over the water towards them. That was queer, very queer. Mr. Quack said so. Mrs. Quack said so. Both were growing more and more suspicious. They couldn't understand it at all, and it is always best to be suspicious of things you cannot understand. Mr. and Mrs. Quack half lifted their wings to fly.

## XXX

# The Mystery Is Solved

IT WAS very mysterious. Yes, Sir, it was very mysterious. Mr. Quack thought so. Mrs. Quack thought so. There, out in the Big River, in the midst of the Black Shadows, was something which looked like the branch of a tree. But instead of moving down the river, as the branch of a tree would if it were floating, this was coming straight across the river as if it were swimming. But how could the branch of a tree swim? That was too much for Mr. Quack. It was too much for Mrs. Quack.

So they sat perfectly still among the brown stalks of the wild rice along the edge of the Big River, and not for a second did they take their eyes from that strange thing moving towards them. They were ready to spring into the air and trust to their swift wings the instant they should detect danger. But they did not want to fly unless they had to. Besides, they were curious. They were very curious indeed. They wanted to find out what that mysterious thing moving through the water towards them was.

So Mr. and Mrs. Quack watched that thing that looked like a swimming branch draw nearer and nearer, and the nearer it drew the more they were puzzled, and the more curious they felt. If it had been the pond of Paddy the Beaver instead of the Big River, they would have thought it was Paddy swimming with a branch for his winter food pile. But Paddy the Beaver was way back in his own pond, deep in the Green Forest, and they knew it. So this thing became more and more of a mystery. The nearer it came, the more nervous and anxious they grew, and at the same time the greater became their curiosity.

At last Mr. Quack felt that not even to gratify his curiosity would it be safe to wait longer. He prepared to spring into the air, knowing that Mrs. Quack would follow him. It was just then that a funny little sound reached him. It was half snort, half cough, as if some one had sniffed some water up his nose. There was something familiar about that sound. Mr. Quack decided to wait a few minutes longer.

"I'll wait," thought Mr. Quack, "until that thing, whatever it is comes out of those Black Shadows into the moonlight. Somehow I have a feeling that we are in no danger."

So Mr. and Mrs. Quack waited and watched. In a few minutes the thing that looked like the branch of a tree came out of the Black Shadows into the moonlight, and then the mystery was solved. It was a mystery no longer. They saw that they had mistaken the antlers of Lightfoot the Deer for the branch of a tree. Lightfoot was swimming across the Big River on his way back to his home in the Green Forest. At once Mr. and Mrs. Quack swam out to meet him and to tell him how glad they were that he was alive and safe.

## XXXI

## A Surprising Discovery

PROBABLY there was no happier Thanksgiving in all the Great World than the Thanksgiving of Lightfoot the Deer, when the dreadful hunting season ended and he was once more back in his beloved Green Forest with nothing to fear. All his neighbors called on him to tell him how glad they were that he had escaped and how the Green Forest would not have been the same if he had not returned. So Lightfoot roamed about without fear and was happy. It seemed to him that he could not be happier. There was plenty to eat and that blessed feeling of nothing to fear. What more could any one ask? He began to grow sleek and fat and handsomer than ever. The days were growing colder and the frosty air made him feel good.

Just at dusk one evening he went down to his favorite drinking place at the Laughing Brook. As he put down his head to drink he saw something which so surprised him that he quite forgot he was thirsty. What do you think it was he saw? It was a footprint in the soft mud. Yes, Sir, it was a footprint.

For a long time Lightfoot stood staring at that footprint. In his great, soft eyes was a look of wonder and surprise. You see, that footprint was exactly like one of his own, only smaller. To Lightfoot it was a very wonderful footprint. He was quite sure that never had he seen such a dainty footprint. He forgot to drink. Instead, he began to search for other footprints, and presently he found them. Each was as dainty as that first one.

Who could have made them? That is what Lightfoot wanted to know and what he meant to find out. It was clear to him that there was a stranger in the Green Forest, and somehow he didn't resent it in the least. In fact, he was glad. He couldn't have told why, but it was true.

Lightfoot put his nose to the footprints and sniffed of them. Even had he not known by looking at those prints that they had been made by a stranger, his nose would have told him this. A great longing to find the maker of those footprints took possession of him. He lifted his handsome head and listened for some slight sound which might show that the stranger was near. With his delicate nostrils he tested the wandering little Night Breezes for a stray whiff of scent to tell him which way to go. But there was no sound and the wandering little Night Breezes told him nothing. Lightfoot followed the dainty footprints up the bank. There they disappeared, for the ground was hard. Lightfoot paused, undecided which way to go.

## XXXII

# Lightfoot Sees the Stranger

LIGHTFOOT the Deer was unhappy. It was a strange unhappiness, an unhappiness such as he had never known before. You see, he had discovered that there was a stranger in the Green Forest, a stranger of his own kind, another Deer. He knew it by dainty footprints in the mud along the Laughing Brook and on the edge of the pond of Paddy the Beaver. He knew it by other signs which he ran across every now and then. But search as he would, he was unable to find that newcomer. He had searched everywhere but always he was just too late. The stranger had been and gone.

Now there was no anger in Lightfoot's desire to find that stranger. Instead, there was a great longing. For the first time in his life Lightfoot felt lonely. So he hunted and hunted and was unhappy. He lost his appetite. He slept little. He roamed about uneasily, looking, listening, testing every Merry Little Breeze, but all in vain.

Then, one never-to-be-forgotten night, as he drank at the Laughing Brook, a strange feeling swept over him. It was the feeling of being watched. Lightfoot lifted his beautiful head and a slight movement caught his quick eye and drew it to a thicket not far away. The silvery light of gentle Mistress Moon fell full on that thicket, and thrust out from it was the most beautiful head in all the Great World. At least, that is the way it seemed to Lightfoot, though to tell the truth it was not as beautiful as his own, for it was uncrowned by antlers. For a

70

long minute Lightfoot stood gazing. A pair of wonderful, great, soft eyes gazed back at him. Then that beautiful head disappeared.

With a mighty bound, Lightfoot cleared the Laughing Brook and rushed over to the thicket in which that beautiful head had disappeared. He plunged in, but there was no one there. Frantically he searched, but that thicket was empty. Then he stood still and listened. Not a sound reached him. It was as still as if there were no other living things in all the Green Forest. The beautiful stranger had slipped away as silently as a shadow.

All the rest of that night Lightfoot searched through the Green Forest but his search was in vain. The longing to find that beautiful stranger had become so great that he fairly ached with it. It seemed to him that until he found her he could know no happiness.

## XXXIII

# A Different Game of Hide and Seek

ONCE MORE Lightfoot the Deer was playing hide and seek in the Green Forest. But it was a very different game from the one he had played just a short time before. You remember that then it had been for his life that he had played, and he was the one who had done all the hiding. Now, he was "it", and some one else was doing the hiding. Instead of the dreadful fear which had filled him in that other game, he was now filled with longing,—longing to find and make friends with the beautiful stranger of whom he had just once caught a glimpse, but of whom every day he found tracks.

At times Lightfoot would lose his temper. Yes, Sir, Lightfoot would lose his temper. That was a foolish thing to do, but it seemed to him that he just couldn't help it. He would stamp his feet angrily and thrash the bushes with his great spreading antlers as if they were an enemy with whom he was fighting. More than once when he did this a pair of great, soft, gentle eyes were watching him, though he didn't know it. If he could have seen them and the look of admiration in them, he would have been more eager than ever to find that beautiful stranger.

At other times Lightfoot would steal about through the Green Forest as noiselessly as a shadow. He would peer into thickets and behind tangles of fallen trees and brush piles, hoping to surprise the one he sought. He would be very, very patient. Perhaps he would come to the thicket which he knew from the signs the stranger had left only a few moments before. Then his patience would vanish in impatience, and he would dash ahead, eager to catch up with the shy stranger. But always it was in vain. He had thought himself very clever but this stranger was proving herself more clever.

Of course it wasn't long before all the little people in the Green Forest knew what was going on. They knew all about that game of hide and seek just as they had known all about that other game of hide and seek with the hunters. But now, instead of trying to help Lightfoot as they did then, they gave him no help at all. The fact is, they were enjoying that game. Mischievous Sammy Jay even went so far as to warn the stranger several times when Lightfoot was approaching. Of course Lightfoot knew when Sammy did this, and each time he lost his temper. For the time being, he quite forgot all that Sammy had done for him when he was the one that was being hunted.

Once Lightfoot almost ran smack into Buster Bear and was so provoked by his own carelessness that instead of bounding away he actually threatened to fight Buster. But when Buster grinned good-naturedly at him, Lightfoot thought better of it and bounded away to continue his search.

Then there were times when Lightfoot would sulk and would declare over and over to himself, "I don't care anything about that stranger. I won't spend another minute looking for her." And then within five minutes he would be watching, listening and seeking some sign that she was still in the Green Forest.

# XXXIV

# A Startling New Footprint

THE GAME of hide and seek between Lightfoot the Deer and the beautiful stranger whose dainty footprints had first started Lightfoot to seeking her had been going on for several days and nights when Lightfoot found something which gave him a shock. He had stolen very softly down to the Laughing Brook, hoping to surprise the beautiful stranger drinking there. She wasn't to be seen. Lightfoot wondered if she had been there, so looked in the mud at the edge of the Laughing Brook to see if there were any fresh prints of those dainty feet. Almost at once he discovered fresh footprints. They were not the prints he was looking for. No, Sir, they were not the dainty prints he had learned to know so well. They were prints very near the size of his own big ones, and they had been made only a short time before.

The finding of those prints was a dreadful shock to Lightfoot. He understood instantly what they meant. They meant that a second stranger had come into the Green Forest, one who had antlers like his own. Jealousy took possession of Lightfoot the Deer; jealousy that filled his heart with rage.

"He has come here to seek that beautiful stranger I have been hunting for," thought Lightfoot. "He has come here to try to steal her away from me. He has no right here in my Green Forest. He belongs back up on the Great Mountain from which he must have come, for there is no other place he could have come from. That is where that beautiful stranger must have come from, too. I want her to stay, but I must drive this fellow out. I'll make him fight. That's what I'll do; I'll make him fight! I'm not afraid of him, but I'll make him fear me."

Lightfoot stamped his feet and with his great antlers thrashed the bushes as if he felt that they were the enemy he sought. Could you have looked into his great eyes then, you would have found nothing soft and beautiful about them. They became almost red with anger. Lightfoot quivered all over with rage. The hair on the back of his neck stood up. Lightfoot the Deer looked anything but gentle.

After he had vented his spite for a few minutes on the harmless, helpless bushes, he threw his head high in the air and whistled angrily. Then he leaped over the Laughing Brook and once more began to search through the Green Forest. But this time it was not for the beautiful stranger with the dainty feet. He had no time to think of her now. He must first find this new-comer and he meant to waste no time in doing it.

## XXXV

# Lightfoot Is Reckless

IN HIS SEARCH for the new stranger who had come to the Green Forest, Lightfoot the Deer was wholly reckless. He no longer stole like a gray shadow from thicket to thicket as he had done when searching for the beautiful stranger with the dainty feet. He bounded along, careless of how much noise he made. From time to time he would stop to whistle a challenge and to clash his horns against the trees and stamp the ground with his feet.

After such exhibitions of anger he would pause to listen, hoping to hear some sound which would tell him where the stranger was. Now and then he found the stranger's tracks, and from them he knew that this stranger was doing just what he had been doing, seeking to find the beautiful newcomer with the dainty feet. Each time he found these signs Lightfoot's rage increased.

Of course it didn't take Sammy Jay long to discover what was going on. There is little that escapes those sharp eyes of Sammy Jay. As you know, he had early discovered the game of hide and seek Lightfoot had been playing with the beautiful young visitor who had come down to the Green Forest from the Great Mountain. Then, by chance, Sammy had visited the Laughing Brook just as the big stranger had come down there to drink. For once Sammy had kept his tongue still. "There is going to be excitement here when

Lightfoot discovers this fellow," thought Sammy. "If they ever meet, and I have a feeling that they will, there is going to be a fight worth seeing. I must pass the word around."

So Sammy Jay hunted up his cousin, Blacky the Crow, and told him what he had discovered. Then he hunted up Bobby Coon and told him. He saw Unc' Billy Possum sitting in the doorway of his hollow tree and told him. He discovered Jumper the Hare sitting under a little hemlock-tree and told him. Then he flew over to the dear Old Briar-patch to tell Peter Rabbit. Of course he told Drummer the Woodpecker, Tommy Tit the Chickadee, and Yank Yank the Nuthatch, who were over in the Old Orchard, and they at once hurried to the Green Forest, for they couldn't think of missing anything so exciting as would be the meeting between Lightfoot and the big stranger from the Great Mountain.

Sammy didn't forget to tell Paddy the Beaver, but it was no news to Paddy. Paddy had seen the big stranger on the edge of his pond early the night before.

Of course, Lightfoot knew nothing about all this. His one thought was to find that big stranger and drive him from the Green Forest, and so he continued his search tirelessly.

## XXXVI
## Sammy Jay Takes a Hand

SAMMY JAY was bubbling over with excitement as he flew about through the Green Forest, following Lightfoot the Deer. He was so excited he wanted to scream. But he didn't. He kept his tongue still. You see, he didn't want Lightfoot to know that he was being followed. Under that pointed cap of Sammy Jay's are quick wits. It didn't take him long to discover that the big stranger whom Lightfoot was seeking was doing his best to keep out of Lightfoot's way and that he was having no difficulty in doing so because of the reckless way in which Lightfoot was searching for him. Lightfoot made so much noise that it was quite easy to know just where he was and so keep out of his sight.

"That stranger is nearly as big as Lightfoot, but it is very plain that he doesn't want to fight," thought Sammy. "He must be a coward."

Now the truth is, the stranger was not a coward. He was ready and willing to fight if he had to, but if he could avoid fighting he meant to. You see, big as he was, he wasn't quite so big as Lightfoot, and he knew it. He had seen Lightfoot's big footprints, and from their size he knew that Lightfoot must be bigger and heavier than he. Then, too, he knew that he really had no right to be there in the Green Forest. That was Lightfoot's home and so he was an intruder. He knew that Lightfoot would feel this way about it and that this would make him fight all the harder. So the big stranger wanted to

78

avoid a fight if possible. But he wanted still more to find that beautiful young visitor with the dainty feet for whom Lightfoot had been looking. He wanted to find her just as Lightfoot wanted to find her, and he hoped that if he did find her, he could take her away with him back to the Great Mountain. If he had to, he would fight for her, but until he had to he would keep out of the fight. So he dodged Lightfoot and at the same time looked for the beautiful stranger.

All this Sammy Jay guessed, and after a while he grew tired of following Lightfoot for nothing. "I'll have to take a hand in this thing myself," muttered Sammy. "At this rate, Lightfoot never will find that big stranger!"

So Sammy stopped following Lightfoot and began to search through the Green Forest for the big stranger. It didn't take very long to find him. He was over near the pond of Paddy the Beaver. As soon as he saw him, Sammy began to scream at the top of his lungs. At once he heard the sound of snapping twigs at the top of a little ridge back of Paddy's pond and knew that Lightfoot had heard and understood.

## XXXVII
# The Great Fight

DOWN FROM the top of the ridge back of the pond of Paddy the Beaver plunged Lightfoot the Deer, his eyes blazing with rage. He had understood the screaming of Sammy Jay. He knew that somewhere down there was the big stranger he had been looking for.

The big stranger had understood Sammy's screaming quite as well as Lightfoot. He knew that to run away now would be to prove himself a coward and forever disgrace himself in the eyes of Miss Daintyfoot, for that was the name of the beautiful stranger he had been seeking. He *must* fight. There was no way out of it, he *must* fight. The hair on the back of his neck stood up with anger just as did the hair on the neck of Lightfoot. His eyes also blazed. He bounded out into a little open place by the pond of Paddy the Beaver and there he waited.

Meanwhile Sammy Jay was flying about in the greatest excitement, screaming at the top of his lungs, "A fight! A fight! A fight!" Blacky the Crow, over in another part of the Green Forest, heard him and took up the cry and at once hurried over to Paddy's pond. Everybody who was near enough hurried there. Bobby Coon and Unc' Billy Possum climbed trees from which they could see and at the same time be safe. Billy Mink hurried to a safe place on the dam of Paddy the Beaver. Paddy himself climbed up on the roof of his house out in the pond. Peter Rabbit and Jumper the Hare, who happened to be not far away, hurried over where they could peep out from under some young hemlock-trees. Buster Bear shuffled down the hill and watched from the other side of the pond. Reddy and Granny Fox were both there.

For what seemed like the longest time, but which was for only a minute, Lightfoot and the big stranger stood still, glaring at each other. Then, snorting with rage, they lowered their heads and plunged together. Their antlers clashed with a noise that rang through the Green Forest, and both fell to their knees. There they pushed and struggled. Then they separated and backed away, to repeat the movement over again. It was a terrible fight. Everybody said so. If they had not known before, everybody knew now what those great antlers were for. Once the big stranger managed to reach Lightfoot's right shoulder with one of the sharp points of his antlers and made a long tear in Lightfoot's gray coat. It only made Lightfoot fight harder.

Sometimes they would rear up and strike with their sharp hoofs. Back and forth they plunged, and the ground was torn up by their feet. Both were getting out of breath, and from time to time they had to stop for a moment's rest. Then they would come together again more fiercely than ever. Never had such a fight been seen in the Green Forest.

## XXXVIII

# An Unseen Watcher

As LIGHTFOOT the Deer and the big stranger from the Great Mountain fought in the little opening near the pond of Paddy the Beaver, neither knew or cared who saw them. Each was filled fully with rage and determined to drive the other from the Green Forest. Each was fighting for the right to win the love of Miss Daintyfoot.

Neither of them knew that Miss Daintyfoot herself was watching them. But she was. She had heard the clash of their great antlers as they had come together the first time, and she had known exactly what it meant. Timidly she had stolen forward to a thicket where, safely hidden, she could watch that terrible fight. She knew that they were fighting for her. Of course. She knew it just as she had known how both had been hunting for her. What she didn't know for some time was which one she wanted to win that fight.

Both Lightfoot and the big stranger were handsome. Yes, indeed, they were very handsome. Lightfoot was just a little bit the bigger and it seemed to her just a little bit the handsomer. She almost wanted him to win. Then, when she saw how bravely the big stranger was fighting and how well he was holding his own, even though he was a little smaller than Lightfoot, she almost hoped he would win.

That great fight lasted a long time. To pretty Miss Daintyfoot it seemed that it never would end. But after a while Lightfoot's greater size and strength began to tell. Little by little the big stranger was forced back towards the edge of the open place. Now he would be thrown to his knees when Lightfoot wasn't. As Lightfoot saw this, he seemed to gain new strength. At last he caught the stranger in such a way that he threw him over. While the stranger struggled to get to his feet again, Lightfoot's sharp antlers made long tears in his gray coat. The stranger was beaten and he knew it. The instant he succeeded in getting to his feet he turned tail and plunged for the shelter of the Green Forest. With a snort of triumph, Lightfoot plunged after him.

But now that he was beaten, fear took possession of the stranger. All desire to fight left him. His one thought was to get away, and fear gave him speed. Straight back towards the Great Mountain from which he had come the stranger headed. Lightfoot followed only a short distance. He knew that that stranger was going for good and would not come back. Then Lightfoot turned back to the open place where they had fought. There he threw up his beautiful head, crowned by its great antlers, and whistled a challenge to all the Green Forest. As she looked at him, Miss Daintyfoot knew that she had wanted him to win. She knew that there simply couldn't be anybody else so handsome and strong and brave in all the Great World.

## XXXIX

## Lightfoot Discovers Love

WONDERFULLY handsome was Lightfoot the Deer as he stood in the little opening by the pond of Paddy the Beaver, his head thrown back proudly, as he received the congratulations of his neighbors of the Green Forest who had seen him win the great fight with the big stranger who had come down from the Great Mountain. To beautiful Miss Daintyfoot, peeping out from the thicket where she had hidden to watch the great fight, Lightfoot was the most wonderful person in all the Great World. She adored him, which means that she loved him just as much as it was possible for her to love.

But Lightfoot didn't know this. In fact, he didn't know that Miss Daintyfoot was there. His one thought had been to drive out of the Green Forest the big stranger who had come down from the Great Mountain. He had been jealous of that big stranger, though he hadn't known that he was jealous. The real cause of his anger and desire to fight had been the fear that the big stranger would find Miss Daintyfoot and take her away. Of course this was nothing but jealousy.

Now that the great fight was over, and he knew that the big stranger was hurrying back to the Great Mountain, all Lightfoot's anger melted away. In its place was a great longing to find Miss Daintyfoot. His great eyes became once more soft and beautiful. In them was a look of wistfulness. Lightfoot walked down to the edge of the water and drank, for he was very, very thirsty. Then he turned, intending to take up once more his search for beautiful Miss Daintyfoot.

When he turned he faced the thicket in which Miss Daintyfoot was hiding. His keen eyes caught a little movement of the branches. A beautiful head was slowly thrust out, and Lightfoot gazed again into a pair of soft eyes which he was sure were the most beautiful eyes in all the Great World. He wondered if she would disappear and run away as she had the last time he saw her.

He took a step or two forward. The beautiful head was withdrawn. Lightfoot's heart sank. Then he bounded forward into that thicket. He more than half expected to find no one there, but when he entered that thicket he received the most wonderful surprise in all his life. There stood Miss Daintyfoot, timid, bashful, but with a look in her eyes which Lightfoot could not mistake. In that instant Lightfoot understood the meaning of that longing which had kept him hunting for her and of the rage which had filled him when he had discovered the presence of the big stranger from the Great Mountain. It was love. Lightfoot knew that he loved Miss Daintyfoot and, looking into her soft, gentle eyes, he knew that Miss Daintyfoot loved him.

## XL

# Happy Days in the Green Forest

THESE WERE happy days in the Green Forest. At least, they were happy for Lightfoot the Deer. They were the happiest days he had ever known. You see, he had won beautiful, slender, young Miss Daintyfoot, and now she was no longer Miss Daintyfoot but Mrs. Lightfoot. Lightfoot was sure that there was no one anywhere so beautiful as she, and Mrs. Lightfoot knew that there was no one so handsome and brave as he.

Wherever Lightfoot went, Mrs. Lightfoot went. He showed her all his favorite hiding-places. He led her to his favorite eating-places. She did not tell him that she was already acquainted with every one of them, that she knew the Green Forest quite as well as he did. If he had stopped to think how day after day she had managed to keep out of his sight while he hunted for her, he would have realized that there was little he could show her which she did not already know. But he didn't stop to think and proudly led her from place to place. And Mrs. Lightfoot wisely expressed delight with all she saw quite as if it were all new.

Of course, all the little people of the Green Forest hurried to pay their respects to Mrs. Lightfoot and to tell Lightfoot how glad they felt for him. And they really did feel glad. You see, they all loved Lightfoot and they knew that now he would be happier than ever, and that there would be no danger of his leaving the Green

Forest because of loneliness. The Green Forest would not be the same at all without Lightfoot the Deer.

Lightfoot told Mrs. Lightfoot all about the terrible days of the hunting season and how glad he was that she had not been in the Green Forest then. He told her how the hunters with terrible guns had given him no rest and how he had had to swim the Big River to get away from the hounds.

"I know," replied Mrs. Lightfoot softly. "I know all about it. You see, there were hunters on the Great Mountain. In fact, that is how I happened to come down to the Green Forest. They hunted me so up there that I did not dare stay, and I came down here thinking that there might be fewer hunters. I wouldn't have believed that I could ever be thankful to hunters for anything, but I am, truly I am."

There was a puzzled look on Lightfoot's face. "What for?" he demanded. "I can't imagine anybody being thankful to hunters for anything."

"Oh, you stupid," cried Mrs. Lightfoot. "Don't you see that if I hadn't been driven down from the Great Mountain, I never would have found *you?*"

"You mean, I never would have found *you*," retorted Lightfoot. "I guess I owe these hunters more than you do. I owe them the greatest happiness I have ever known, but I never would have thought of it myself. Isn't it queer how things which seem the very worst possible sometimes turn out to be the very best possible?"

Blacky the Crow is one of Lightfoot's friends, but sometimes even friends are envious. It is so with Blacky. He insists that he is quite as important in the Green Forest as is Lightfoot and that his doings are quite as interesting. Therefore just to please him the next book is to be Blacky the Crow.

# CHILDREN'S THRIFT CLASSICS

Paperbound unless otherwise indicated. Available at your book dealer, online at **www.doverpublications.com**, or by writing to Dept. 23, Dover Publications, Inc., 31 East 2nd Street, Mineola, NY 11501. For current price information or for free catalogs (please indicate field of interest), write to Dover Publications or log on to **www.doverpublications.com** and see every Dover book in print. Each year Dover publishes over 500 books on fine art, music, crafts and needlework, antiques, languages, literature, children's books, chess, cookery, nature, anthropology, science, mathematics, and other areas.

*Manufactured in the U.S.A.*